soulslut

mooshe

Columbus, Ohio
empbooks.com

First Edition:10 19 33 34 6 11 1973
ISBN: 979-8-88596-199-8
LOC: 2022931842
Design, Layout, and Edits: Ezhno Martín
Photos: Mooshe

Attempts to identify. Those are scarier than a mugshot.

Escaped inmate? Newly booked sex offender? The Shroud of Turin gives me the same primal chill. Maybe because I believed in aliens and spontaneous combustion as a kid ... walking a dog alone at night in a nice neighborhood you are only allowed to be afraid of aliens and God.

A mugshot is clear. Crisp. An attempt to identify is just a shadow from a surveillance cam.

Who could even identity a friend or a family member or neighbor from that kind of video? I couldn't.

I cannot identify myself most days.

Outside of the neurotic thought patterns that comfort me I don't know who I am or what I could be. My entire existence is constantly threatening to float away.

Getting high and riding shotgun and poking
his face to Tom DeLonge because
it's the sexiest voice paired with the
sexiest boy. I poke the mole on his face.
He has a straight-up movie-star pin-up
girl beauty-mark because he's my perfect
girlfriend and I am very lucky.

He cooked me dinner tonight.

We kissed in the kitchen. We discussed
language as a virus and Gauguin. I'm going
down HARD. So hard that on the drive home
I was feeling transcendent listening to
U2. Love shouldn't do that to people.

He's going to kill me.
It's OK. We might be OK.

We've had time to come to terms with the
scary stuff before we were emotionally
invested. Nevertheless this is a
Backstreet Boys-sized crush.

It is super fucked up when someone tells a girl they're not looking for a relationship but then they buy another girl flowers... then dinner then flowers then repeat for another girl and another during the 18 months the first girl has known him.

I haven't been able to open myself to another person in years.

I learned everything I know about Frank Zappa watching documentaries naked and alone in a stranger's bed after he left for work.

This situation is **"*Your House'ing*"** defined by a very personal and deeply hidden track off Jagged Little Pill.

Our most personal and mortifying experiences are not universal.

Queens New York in an apartment above someone else's home. Recently divorced with ceilings short and vaulted - that's also how I would describe his height and the type of acrobatics I performed on his body.

It was a big date. Our third date. The date I let him tell me his 9/11 story. Of course I'm someone that fucks before the third date but I need some time before you tell me where you were when your ex-wife did not die in 9/11.

We had sex with the window open. It was summer and it was beautiful. Do not mistake this for a romantic evening.

Here's a power-move you learn from the scumbags in their 30s that you date in your 20s:

Keep a coffee maker next to your bed. You live alone. Who is going to bitch at you about starting a fire? It's why you smoke in bed too. You make coffee and light a cigarette before you open your eyes.

Do not lie to me. No one can make coffee and smoke a cigarette before getting up to pee. Just hit up the kitchen you lazy fuck.

I'm going to work. Let yourself out.

I didn't do that part. I watched his videos. I ate English muffins. I took a shower. The bathroom was smaller than a closet. Today I know showers with toilets inside exist. My memory has me believing his bathroom was this way. Things weren't like that back then.

Would you forgive me love? He pays for cable. **Would you forgive me love if I laid in your bed?** I put on another Zappa documentary. I'm out immediately and for seven hours. **Would you forgive me love if I stay all afternoon?**

Waking up in a panic is universal.

Your alarm didn't go off. Your kids let you sleep in late, so obviously they are dead now. The phone rang — who the hell is calling you at this hour?! But to wake up after the sun has set in someone's bachelor pad? You're a fucking idiot.

Truthfully I didn't wake up in that moment that exact moment of his keys in the door. I was awake when he hit the driveway like that psycho psychic shit dogs do. I had the luxury of a moment on my own to panic. **What have I done?!** He probably knew that. He didn't have that luxurious moment alone but I can't be the only person to know that.

But... he saw me again. He let me stay in his bed through the night. We ate his favorite pizza at a table and he told me which two teeth were rotting out of his head. He's only 34. I think it's sweet.

This date was a big date too. Our fourth date — the date he taught me how to use a bus. Infantalizing at worst and necessary at best.

If you see something, say something! Does the MTA still use that slogan? ***If you see something, say something!*** ***DAAAAAAYUUUUUMMMMMMNN!***

I left late again and the bus had just picked up the high school kids. My Walk of Shame meets Hall of Fame:

NICE TITS DAAAAYHUUUUMMM!

The worst part about getting to fuck a guy once - maybe twice - is that you ruin the memory immediately. You access it too many times. You rewrote it before it had a chance to build itself into the cellular structure of your brain. You've changed something subtle and adorable into something dramatic and weird. All the times you muscled him around or the big finish. Those aren't the good moments. Those aren't the ways he talks with just his lips, keeping his mouth mostly shut.

All my good sex stories involve strangers or puking or crying.

I fucked the dirtiest heroin addict on our team. I made him get in a car at 3am and drive me to Maryland to do it there. We put porn on the TV. We were already blacked out and we were already fucking. What a waste. Fucking idiots.

I bet we didn't use a condom.

There was a guy who tried to kill himself on our date.

I am fucking poison. The most scandalous
sex story I can tell is a group sex story
but group sex is boring. More people —
more parts. The only thing that really
sticks with me and burns me and makes
me sick to my stomach with rage and
regret is that the wife got mad at me
for bruising her ankles.

Is this the root of my jealousy?
Baby's first manic pixie poison? It was
consensual. It was fine. I apologized.
She brought milk and cookies into bed. I
broke them up. No. Jay brought the milk
and cookies. Jay broke them up. When we
fucked in the hotel room on every single
surface against the 57th floor window and
titty-fucked for the first time was the
cheating. I was a jerk about the ankles
and a jerk about the cheating.

This cheap Dollar Store cookie in one
reluctant bite.

Seventeen days. That's how long it takes between having sex and when Star Trek is interesting again. They don't teach you that in sex-ed. That's something you learn in the field.

I learned this six months into a three year break-up.

I spent a large chunk of my twenties in a long distance relationship. I wasn't holding out for marriage or anything. I don't believe in marriage. I mean, obviously! Well obviously marriage is a real thing in this physical world – but why? For who? People who can't write individual contracts? How can you really only have one person in your life? Only one ready to decide when to pull the plug on the ventilator while also watching you, waiting for you to overdraw the checking account? I can do one of those things myself and the other one by downloading a living will.

Or with a tattoo.

D.N.R.

I'm not a romantic but I spent my twenties in a long distance relationship. We went from fucking twice a day everyday to every two weeks. Every six weeks.

Whenever one of us wasn't working.

Whenever I felt like driving to Connecticut.

He waited on bus schedules. It was very practical. I would feel fear in my entire body and mistake it for the need to get fucked and drive to Connecticut. I didn't have money for gas in those days. Why would I drive 100 miles for a commitment?

<u>WHY</u>: It was nice not to think about sex. It was nice not to think about everyone I met naked. Have you ever fucked a friend just to stop having dreams about their micro-penis? I'm not proud of it but I am proud to report his penis is fine. Halfhearted requests for me to stop. You're already inside. His live lives abroad. I don't believe in marriage. Is that why I keep trying to destroy them? I don't seek it out. Who is doing this to me?

Tell me the steps I took in life to be driving on country roads consistently at 2am. Every day is the longest day ever, and they all go by so fast. I have no sense of life more than three weeks from now, and I'm so open to anything that each year feels like a rebellion against the last. Did one decision lead me here or is this just a long misunderstanding?

I am lonely. My best friends are scattered across the country and it makes me feel warm until I realize every move I make is completely alone. I move around a lot, and when I do, I carry my own mattress and couch and drive my own rented truck. Does this make me fiercely independent or a fucking idiot?

I get older and everyone wants to be married or already had children and I have become a proxy for something I know nothing about. I don't think anyone has ever fought their ego long enough to figure out that I am being sincere when I say I have no expectations and don't want anything. I am down for everything. I'm easygoing but with a lot of intensity. I'm sorry if you see the intensity. It might be a carryover from working so hard for so long with nothing to show for it. It might be a poorly developed shadow-self. That bitch is a fucking nightmare. She's never had to negotiate bad behavior with anyone else. Because ... why? I have never done anything I didn't want to do except be awake right now. I don't want to be this tired and wired driving for hours when everyone else is in bed after a long night out with their safety net.

These are just survival instincts.

I'm watching him blackout drunk on the couch having the worst night terrors I've ever seen. For a moment it feels like a bonfire. And not because he moves and lashes like tendrils of flame. For a moment I am at peace and not alone and in darkness. Remember this next time feelings creep up on you.

No. Don't. This is exactly what we're afraid of. I can in this moment feel myself grown old – too old – older than I've ever wanted to be. In this moment the chaos of the universe feels more familiar than the silence or the stopping to feel. The hum of the fridge is a memory old as time. I was born with that sound fueling fear in every part of my body even though it's a quiet noise.

It's everywhere.

If you squint you can see rays of light drawn with crayon radiating from the kitchen.

There's that scene in Mad Men where Sally is watching her dad shave. Her dad is John Hamm when it strikes you: ***Damn. That girl is going to be into some weird shit someday.***

My boyfriend shaves his legs.

His arms and face and stray hairs on his chest and shoulders. He wears my Chanel perfume and my clothes and we are the exact same age. I do not have Daddy Issues.

I do not have Daddy Issues.

I do not have Daddy Issues.

I say it again and again because when your dad dies before your eighteenth birthday everyone expects you to have Daddy Issues.

On Saturdays in the summer my family would order pizza. It's always 20 minutes and my dad and I leave 18 minutes too early. We stop at the liquor store. I watch him smoke a couple cigarettes. I don't think we talk the entire time. I press the pizza box in my lap. These are the last days of the last summer I can wear shorts. I'm unconsciously trying to see if I get third degree burns before we make it all the way home. Maybe if I get burns I'll never have to shave my legs.

Fun fact: Girls cannot wear shorts once men begin to notice them. No one explained this to me, just called me a fat fucking whore. ***NOT IN MY HOUSE. Get out of my house! You can make money by walking the streets.***

Thanks Mom.

You fucking bitch.

It's the second week in a row that I am
violently throwing up NY-style pizza and
Four Loko at three in the morning. If
I do anything more than once it feels
like a routine. My entire world starts
to fall in on itself. I get sucked into
my anxiety. If you do anything more than
once you're better off dead.
Early in a relationship my entire body
fights any and every routine. If something
is working my body goes into overdrive
so we aren't happy and can't be a real
couple because we aren't married. I don't
want to be married. I don't want him to
think about his ex-wife when he looks at
me. I want him to see who I am. I want
to breathe between sentences.

Please.

Remember you're in the shower now. This
headache is ridiculous. Thinking should
scratch it out like a bad lotto ticket.
Just drop it. See? No prize.

**I'm dying. I've been poisoned.
This can't be me.**

My body wants me to live — live life to the fullest. Feel every bruise and make sure it is the brightest blue and sharpest pain. Otherwise what do you have to show for yourself? Are you forcing your boyfriend to repeat the same patterns he did with his wife? That's reason enough to vomit all night. Reject that idea. Throw it out of your body. Or are you just poisoned by the algae toxins of Lake Erie?

I've been convinced that heavy metals have soaked through my hair into my skull and are killing me.

THE TRUTH:

DO NOT DRINK FOUR LOKO.
DO NOT EAT BAD PIZZA.
DO NOT LOOK INTO HIS PAST.

Puke your guts out in the shower. Keep washing it out of your hair. Flush it down the toilet before you catch a smell. More warm water. More soap. Warm water is nicer than lake water.

Is this mindfulness?

We sat on the rocks and tempted fate by crawling to the side that forms a natural barrier. I felt close to him in that moment. We're not. We're dangerously on the edge of no longer being separate people.

The pollution or toxins or bacteria have made its way into our brains and have started ***The Break Up*** process early. I'm sorry. It's not me. I'm sick from a parasite. The parasite is my lover. My parasite is me. We know how to swim but it was dumb to crawl past the jetties.

We're on the rocks — not the relationship rocks or the liquor rocks but the lake rocks. I am stuck on these rocks. In this lake. This poisonous lake. It gets more poisonous in summer, you know?

We're on the rocks and we are close and
we are beautiful and no one is falling
and no one is getting crushed by the
waves. It takes straight liquor and rocks
to bring us together as we desperately
fight to hold hands without fusing into
the same person.

The puking helps. If your entire body
rejects this commitment you will be
yourself again by sunrise.

I cried because I didn't get to cum.

Not come to the party not come to the
table not come to the show. I'm crying
because I did not cum.

Was he always a selfish lover? I'm sober
tonight. Am I always a drunk lover? I
busted his lip. He called me mean. He
had me pinned on the wall with my legs
wrapped around his back and I pushed him
back to the bed and he threw a fit. You
fucking cunt. He didn't say that yet. He
hate-fucked me first then ghosted me for a
week. He told me he has a girlfriend now.

That was before. Today I can't cum and I hate him for being afraid of me. Maybe there's something to that argument. He's had a heart attack. I could give him another just because I desperately want to fuck him more than once a week.

You're a bitch in bed and you know it. All the sex you have can can be taken out of context or taken in the context of the other person's perspective in such a way that makes you a monster and can ruin your life.

You are a woman so this cannot be true.

No no! I didn't ask if I could do some Spiderman-shit on his dick. I laughed when he smacked me. He broadcast our first blowjob on Chatroullete.

That's not on me. He didn't ask. We never ask. Our evil is mutual. Why isn't that enough?

I don't cum.

I feel bad.

I walk myself out and see ropes on the couch. I come back. I bang on the door. He's not happy to see me again but I want to know about the ropes. **Who were you fucking before me?** Like... **RIGHT BEFORE ME.** You were wearing shoes when I came in. Those are some fancy knots in those ropes. **Who the hell did you fuck?**

I took out the trash and came back in screaming. He said those ropes were for his bike. Nancy Drew would have asked **WHO THE HELL TIES THEIR BIKE UP WITH ROPE.** Not me. I'm an idiot and it takes me days to figure that one out. Too trusting. Too gullible. Just tell me the truth so I don't get trich from your dick. Again.

I want to die. I tell him I want to die. I start to cry because I want to die. Or cum. I don't know. He puts Vitamin B12 drops under my tongue like a baby bird and sends me on my way.

We Can Not Fuck Again.

Duh.

Oh my god did you think I didn't know that? Of course I know that! Let me apologize for my behavior before you tell me something so obvious! Cannot fuck again!

I know I know I know I am poison.

You don't know. You weren't there at work today when the only way to survive was to count the time between suicidal thoughts like seconds between lighting and thunder.

I take pictures at graduations.

Hundreds of students file through my line. I want to die. That was three students. I wish I could kill myself. Ten students. Why won't I die? Five students. I just want to die. Ten students. I want to die. Ten students.

I want to die. Ten students. I see it has evened out. I guess if it's not going to go away it might as well be predictable.

I'm not ready for a relationship.

What does that mean? *I'm not in a place to be in a relationship.* What does that mean? *I don't want to be in a relationship.* **WHAT THE FUCK DOES IT MEAN?** I've heard it so many times it has no meaning. Someone please define a relationship because all I'm looking for is sex more than twice a week. Just more than twice. Just regular intervals. Every six months. Every three months in between your three month girlfriends. Every time it rains. Fuck me every time it rains. Every time I drink. I'm sorry if I drink a lot. Just give me some boundaries and I'll fuck off.

I just want to fuck. Ten students. **I want to fuck.** Ten students. **I just want to fuck.** That's why we rolled a massive blunt in your kitchen and we got so high I admitted to you that I couldn't tell my best friend's kid I love her. A fucking four year old kid can't hear the words "I love you" because I don't know what love is.

What's his side of this disaster story?
Will he ever write it in a self-important
#METOO essay? Oh bro, this dumb cunt was
a 'digger alright... instead of gold,
though, all I wanted was to know what
it feels like to be old, secure, high,
and in the captain's seat of this house.
Holy shit I understand my feng shui!

He has a beautiful elaborate pencil drawing
of his beautiful Jewish mother when she
was young. A soft and generous portrait
from a starving artist just looking to
make rent. Framed in plated gold. Instead
of hanging it on the wall it sits on the
floor against the wall of a living room
otherwise empty but for two guitars and a
bicycle. He says his stuff is upstairs in
the apartment being remodeled. These are
just a few things that make him happy.
I sneak peeks of his mom every time he
disappears to the bathroom to pee. I
don't know what it's like to want your mom
around like that in a room where you're
finishing a entire bottle of Johnny Walker
watching someone do yoga in the nude.

He gets me high. I alternate between
smoking pot and sucking his cock and I
hold the pipe and his penis both in front
of my lips at once and switch back and
forth until it feels like I'm flying.

This is the first time in my life my
thoughts aren't there.

Is this how normal people live?

I stay over. He is kind about it. I take
my time then take the bus to the subway.
I immediately find his porn collection.
Under the porn collection he has these
little books.

Making Your Dreams Come True!
The Best Way to Plan Your Day!
Success Without Regret!

Sincere and corny. I think the typefaces
go back to 1979. I am now in love. I
don't know if it is with him or with his
things.

I get left home again.

Sleep in! Watch movies! No, read the little books. I missed a detail. The publisher is Catholic. He is always bragging about sleeping with his Hebrew school teacher. Catholicism only comes up in conversations about his ex-wife. This is stolen property! I'm more in love. Maybe this was a spiteful snatch:

You ruined my life? I'll keep you from putting yours back together!

Maybe it's just sentimental. A memory of a marriage that was too stupid to make it without Six Attitudes for Winners. Obviously they never read the book together otherwise they'd still be winning.

What if touching a man's bookshelf is a boundary girlfriends aren't supposed to push? Someone out there is writing a thinkpiece right now about how traumatizing it was that I saw their marked up copy of Infinite Jest.

One time after work everyone got drunk. Strike that. We always drank after work. This time I was told I could crash in his bed. I don't know if I was handsy but I was drunk and I rolled over to sleep and I woke up to **Just The Tip**. This is not rape. I took care of it. Told him to fuck off then and there. End of story.

This is not a story I am telling for your movement.

He hated the first time we had sex.

We were together for years but he always hated that I was drunk and came in from the other room with no pants, all thong. I guess we had stupid stupid stupid bad drunk sex that made him feel like less of a man.

I touched a dick today. I wasn't into it. Is it me? Did I grow up? Was it a bad dick? Is this love?

Two down blankets and four pillows. A quiet movie. Sleeping alone for twelve hours. Remember this feeling the next time you want to text him.

Captains Log: I can no longer count how many days he's been in my home. I'll starting to feel calm which is exactly how you get comfortable and end up dead. I feel a million shitty things floating in my fucking nonsense head. ***Do. Not. Die. Here. Do. Not. Let. Him. Age. You.*** He is going to wake up one day and resent you for all the 20-somethings he didn't fuck because he was perfectly happy passed out drunk on your couch. When this happens ***DO. NOT. BLAME. YOURSELF.***

Except maybe do. Your shadow-self keeps escaping. You hurled a pint glass thru the kitchen window.

Instead of fighting we packed our clothes and all our beers and took off South on a highway until we couldn't remember who we were anymore. I barfed out the backseat window. He tried to steal corn. We don't know how we got... wherever we ended up.

...it was far away.

Why were we fighting all the time? You are fighting yourself, you fucking idiot.

Establishing Boundaries: An expert might tell you to do this right away but when you've commitment adverse perhaps it is best to start with all defenses down. See which ones build up the quickest. The scar tissue that doesn't form is the boundaries you were wrong about.

Let's get a puppy!

Just kidding! I'm still warming up to the idea of a coffee maker in my kitchen.

I never saw my dad in the kitchen unless it was for four fingers of whiskey. My mom used to mark my dad's whiskey bottles to see if he was drunk. Weird. You'd think if you were married to someone you could tell. I can always tell when my boyfriend's been drinking. His skin is warmer and softer and he's already the warmest person I know. His skin vibrates and he would bury his face under my skin if he could.

I hear stories of my dad riding motorcycles and racing sailboats and flying planes before I was born. There is a classic car in the garage. A '37 Plymouth with brown vinyl seats. I remember the steering wheel being as large as my body. Was I two or three?

I have three memories of my dad. Only one where that car came out of the garage. It stayed parked with Christmas presents in the trunk for 20-some years.

We didn't celebrate Christmas. My mom took it away but she hoarded the toys in the trunk of the Plymouth. There were Barbies. I know because when she'd leave us home alone and I would sneak out there and look at what we were missing out on. I never stole a single toy.

One time my dad actually turned the car around on a day trip to a Christmas Dystopia called Frankenmuth.

When you imagine a family vacation, do you imagine an **All Or Nothing** weekend trapped in the backseat with your brothers? Or sharing a hotel room with a sulking mom?

My family didn't know anything about having fun. We were in a museum with blue plastic plaques about Watergate. Nixon and Watergate! Just for fun!

A place called Bronner's that's all Christmas all the time. I wonder if my mom was entertaining the idea of letting us have the holiday back?

But we fucked that up.

Something happened. I don't remember. I
can't remember last week so definitely
not 1990-whatever. The car was either
shouting or silent — both were used as
weapons in our home.

Dad drove us back home. One hour. The
longest hour of my life. A huge investment
had been sank.

Now I drive an hour just for one drink
with a dull Tinder date.

I can't tell you how many people I have
slept with but I can tell you their
nicknames. Cancer Boy. Cancer Wife. Text
Message Boyfriend. Ginger Bro.

Mustache...

No.

Not that.

What was his nickname?

We made out outside when he left to smoke. We made out at the bar. Oh my god! I'm not very original. I get mad at lovers for asking me to fill the roles of previous women but here I am!

We drive in circles. We make out in my car in an office park. Just like teenagers. We Netflix and Chill. He has a Charlie Chaplin tattoo that looks like Hitler. That should have been his nickname.

Fast forward two years.

Hey. Hey. So I've gained 35 pounds in break-up weight and I'm really sorry for what I did. I was kind of a dick and you didn't deserve to be treated that way.

He's right. I didn't deserve to be treated that way. I had left my scarf at his place and the night I came by for it with the promise of hand stuff I knocked on his door. Nothing. I text. And nothing. I text. Still nothing. I pick up the phone and call him which is something only crazy bitches do. I hear the ringing through the walls. I hear myself being ghosted in real time. ***35 pounds in break-up weight.*** I get it dude! Do you think you're the first guy to tell me you were too stoned or too dumb or too scared to see me one night?

We go out again. Not because his pitch was particularly strong but because it was happening again. Someone else was falling in love with someone else behind my back.

To my surprise everything we did was cute.

Wait. Make that a headline.

To My Surprise
Everything We Did Was Cute

He came to my show and passed me a note
You look great tonight. We made out in
my car. He cooked me dinner after making
out next to the bell peppers. We held
hands in the checkout and it was only a
little bit gross.

I get a head start drinking and he meets
me at the bar. I see him and immediately
want to fuck. I'm 15 miles from home and
he's 15 in the opposite direction but he
wants to fix this problem and drive my
ass around. A thirty minute drive and a
40 second pee... I come in for a kiss.

He's really sorry.

His friend needs him. His friend needs
him to bail them out of jail. Friends
are important. Do I wait up? No. Put
your shoes on. Go home.

Miss Nancy Drew did you see it first?

When he held my hand and said *Drunk Mooshe is cute and cuddly and Regular Mooshe is not* ... did you know how shitty that was? I didn't question a they/them pronoun from a two-genders kind of guy. I bet you did, Miss Drew.

I didn't read his texts or look over his shoulder. I figured this one out on my own.

His name was CJ. He died back in May when a car crossed the center line. He bailed his favorite ex-girlfriend out of jail while we were on a date.

Everyone has the one they'd do anything for except me. I'd do anything for anyone which means I'm the one that gets dropped off at my car. Too drunk to drive home. This was the best story the bartender heard all week so I got my Red Bull for free.

Did you know I didn't even block him? I even asked him for a follow-up. Get this! Her dad bailed her out of jail before he even got there.

The fuck?! This girl has an ex-boyfriend that loves her and a dad too? The fuck? The fuck am I doing to myself?! The fuck. The fucking fuck.

December my senior year I had decided this year I wasn't going to wear a winter coat anymore. There was something grounding about wearing a thin green jacket with punk patches and pins year round when it wasn't even strong enough to protect me from air conditioning. It had just snowed so we walked in the street. My sister and I next to two police cars from the next suburb over.

We laughed: *Ooh, Redford police. What are they doing here? Are they looking for drugs? Hey pigs! We got so many drugs! Come back and take our drugs, officers!*

For the record we didn't have drugs. Kids in these suburbs OD on heroin twice before they turn 15 but I was straight edge.

No sex. No drugs. No missing out.

I saw so many dicks back then!

All my friends showed me their dicks.
Kids these days don't whip out their
limp dicks like they used to. They don't
tuck them between their legs and chase
you around naked in the woods screaming
quotes from Dr. Frankenfuter.

There are more beats to this story.

There have to be more beats than this.

Too bad the thing I remember next is being
in a hospital getting hugged by nuns.

My dad died in a car crash.

A nun held me against my will against
a fucking Christmas sweatershirt and my
dad died in a car crash.

Not even a real nun! She's just wearing
a regular person's sweatshirt!

Everyone says I have to see the body.

You have to see the body.

It's not even a good sweatshirt it's not
funny or anything.

You're going to change your mind someday.
Go see the body.

It could at least have embroidered Jesus
on it or something.

But go see your dad as a group. Make it
a family fucking field trip.

Because you might fucking change your
mind someday!

*Other things other people say you are
going to change your mind about include*

Having kids.

Cutting your hair.

Being gay.

Moving away.

Making out with your coworker.

FUN FACT: my body picks a fight with my lover every time it ovulates. It so deeply fears having a baby I scream and cry like one once a month. My body is obsessed with his pheromones. I sleep with my face in his armpits 23 days a month but for one week the chemicals in my body wage war with the man I love because he is an unfit father. It isn't fair. I don't even want kids.

Being a woman isn't fair. Nothing is fair. I cry all the time that life isn't fair.

Mostly in private, but the people close to me see it when I'm screaming it and hate me for it. I'm furious about everything. I try to keep it to myself and apologize and reflect but in college my favorite story was that a boy I called over for sex walked four miles to get to me at three in the morning. He jumped a fence because I was passed out and missed seven calls. I woke up long enough to blow him ... but all my front teeth were broken and jagged little pills from driving y moped into a parking gate. That's a blowjob you have nightmares about for the rest of your life.

I loved that story. I thought it was so funny. It was funny and sweet and it boosted my stupid fucking ego because a cute boy went through a lot of bullshit for me.

Now that story is a demon.

I'm on the wrong side of a movement. An entire movement for women to feel safer but I was doing it wrong this whole time. I was the one causing the trauma. How can I feel like a victim and a monster all at the same time? Every single day. It comes out everyday and I'm the only traitor to women. No one else has ever done evil shit.

SOLUTION: STOP FUCKING AROUND.

Stop hurting people. I'm not sure it's working. A dude stopped talking to me after I said no to butt stuff. I saw him get back together with his ex-girlfriend. All I wanted to do for weeks was send Amazon butt plugs to their house. I know where he lived. It'd be easy and funny and mean.

I have almost scrubbed the place of his memory. I did it almost as quickly as I scrubbed my place of my cat. Worst of any story is when my cat died I threw the body out in the trash. I couldn't help it. It was garbage day and I didn't have 200 bucks for cremation. 150 for the vet to figure it out. They just gave me the body back and didn't stop me. I did wrap his body nicely with the euthanasia papers and his toys but it's not like I could put him in the ground at my apartment complex. He won't tell me where he lives because he doesn't feel safe around me but he left his toothbrush. Not the toothbrush we shared but his toothbrush. He wouldn't even let me have my own toothbrush how am I the one that **Wanted** to be in a **Relationship?**

His head smelled so sweet the days leading up to the breakup. I wondered if this is what women mean when they said a newborn baby's head smells so sweet.

I didn't think it was testosterone electrifying his body and telegraphing to me that he was already on the move out of my life.

I didn't think that I'd have to move.

Shut it down and leave the city is my break-up style.

I wanted to think that moving away from home and sucking cock was the normal thing. That moving away from home and getting your pussy touched to Batman Beyond or Harold and Kumar go to White Castle or Me Myself and Irene are all just normal parts of being a teen.

I still think it's normal.

Getting my pussy ate is the most normal thing about me.

I can only identify myself in these
stories but not the men. When you date
the same losers over and over they lose
their shape and life loses its meaning.
When all you want to feel is every cell in
your body vibrate at a higher frequency
it's easy to get dragged over and over
again with someone easy to take to bed.

Someday there will be nothing left to
destroy. Women age out of the system.
These men keep playing these games and
the shitty slutty women eventually drink
tea and become vanity novelists.